MW01236054

SPACE
MYSTERIES

COULD AN ASTEROID HARM EARTH?

Gareth Stevens
Publishing

BY MICHAEL PORTMAN

Please visit our website, www.garethstevens.com. For a free color catalog of all our high-quality books, call toll free 1-800-542-2595 or fax 1-877-542-2596.

Library of Congress Cataloging-in-Publication Data

Portman, Michael, 1976-
 Could an asteroid harm earth? / Michael Portman.
     p. cm. — (Space mysteries)
 Includes index.
 ISBN 978-1-4339-8268-2 (pbk.)
 ISBN 978-1-4339-8269-9 (6-pack)
 ISBN 978-1-4339-8267-5 (library binding)
 1. Asteroids—Collisions with Earth—Juvenile literature. I. Title.
 QB651.P67 2013
 363.34'9—dc23
                            2012022060

First Edition

Published in 2013 by
Gareth Stevens Publishing
111 East 14th Street, Suite 349
New York, NY 10003

Copyright © 2013 Gareth Stevens Publishing

Designer: Katelyn E. Reynolds
Editor: Therese Shea

Photo credits: Cover, p. 1 alin b./Shutterstock.com; cover, pp. 1, 3–32 (background texture) David M. Schrader/ Shutterstock.com; pp. 3–32 (fun fact graphic) © iStockphoto.com/spxChrome; p. 5 Digital Vision/Thinkstock.com; p. 7 StockTrek Images/Getty Images; p. 9 MarcelClemens/Shutterstock.com; p. 11 Jerry Schad/Photo Researchers/Getty Images; p. 13 D. Van Ravenswaay/Science Photo Library/Getty Images; p. 15 StockTrek Images/Thinkstock.com; p. 17 Mark Garlick/Science Photo Library/Getty Images; p. 19 Wknight94/Wikipedia.com; pp. 20, 21 iStockphoto/Thinkstock.com; p. 23 Adastra/Taxi/Getty Images; p. 25 NASA/JPL-Caltech/UMD via Getty Images; p. 27 Detlev van Ravenswaay/Picture Press/ Getty Images; p. 29 NASA/JPL-Caltech.

Printed in the United States of America

CPSIA compliance information: Batch #CW13GS: For further information contact Gareth Stevens, New York, New York at 1-800-542-2595.

CONTENTS

Words in the glossary appear in **bold** type the first time they are used in the text.

EMPTY SPACE?

Space can certainly seem pretty empty, but it's not. It's full of **debris**, and Earth is constantly running into objects. Every day, Earth gets hit by more than 100 tons (91 t) of rocks and metal from space!

Thankfully, most of the debris that hits Earth isn't very big. It's usually smaller than a grain of sand. We don't have to worry about something that small. But what about something bigger? Could it harm Earth? First, let's take a closer look at all this space junk!

OUT OF THIS WORLD!

One hundred tons is roughly equal to the weight of 50 cars! That sounds like a lot, but compared to the size of Earth, it's actually pretty small.

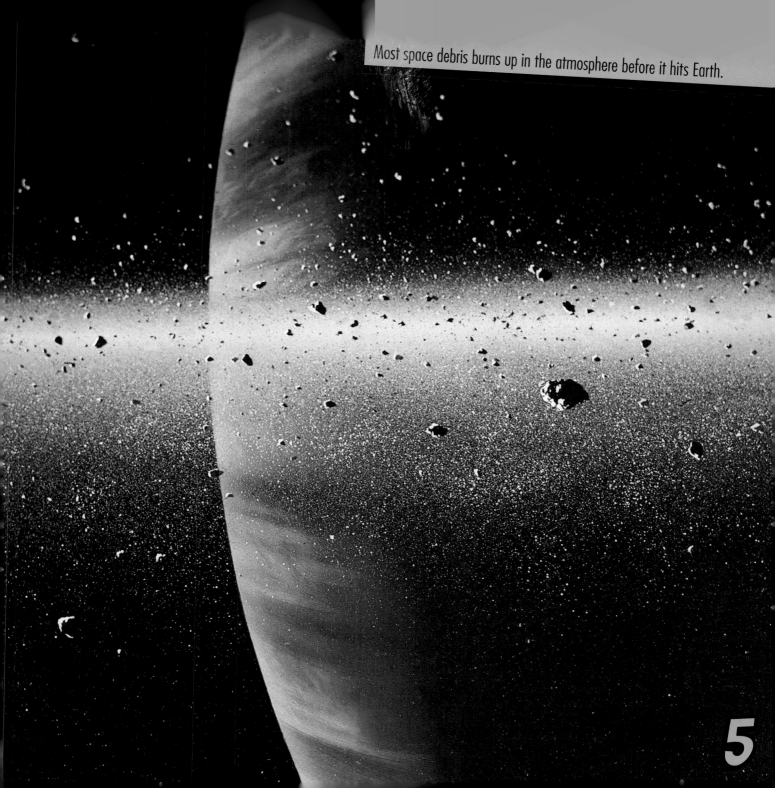

Most space debris burns up in the atmosphere before it hits Earth.

5

WHAT ARE ASTEROIDS?

Asteroids are pieces of rock or metal in space. They range in size from a few feet to several miles wide. Most asteroids **orbit** the sun between Mars and Jupiter in an area called the asteroid belt. There might be billions of asteroids, but, so far, **astronomers** have only found a small fraction.

Not all asteroids are located in the asteroid belt. Some have different orbits that bring them close to Earth. The **gravity** of other planets can sometimes cause asteroids to change course and head toward Earth.

OUT OF THIS WORLD!

Asteroids fall into two categories: solid rocks or metal and rubble piles. Rubble piles are many smaller asteroids held together by gravity.

The first asteroid—and the largest that we know of—was discovered in 1801. It's named Ceres and is roughly 600 miles (965 km) across.

METEOROIDS AND COMETS

Meteoroids are basically small asteroids. Meteoroids are created when asteroids collide, or crash together, and break apart. If a meteoroid reaches the surface of a planet or moon, it's called a meteorite.

Comets are balls made of rock and ice. They're nicknamed "dirty snowballs"! A comet's orbit may change when it passes near giant planets, such as Neptune, Uranus, Saturn, and Jupiter. The gravities of these planets "tug" on comets. This makes it hard for scientists to know the path of a comet.

OUT OF THIS WORLD!

Comet Shoemaker-Levy 9 smashed into Jupiter in July 1994. It broke into pieces before **impact**, and scientists were able to watch these collide with Jupiter.

When a comet gets close to the sun, some of its ice melts. The melting ice gives off gas and dust, which is what gives a comet its tail.

SHOOTING STARS

Have you ever seen a shooting star in the night sky? What we call shooting stars aren't really stars at all. They're actually meteoroids that fall into Earth's atmosphere. Astronomers call the trail of light the meteoroid creates as it falls a meteor.

Where does the light come from? The meteoroid is moving very, very fast—up to 45 miles (72 km) per second. **Friction** between the meteoroid and matter in the atmosphere produces great heat. This causes the meteoroid to burn up and give off light as it falls.

OUT OF THIS WORLD!

Small meteoroids usually burn up farther than 50 miles (80 km) above us.

10

space object	definition
asteroid	a medium to large chunk of rock or metal
meteoroid	a small asteroid or other small object in space
comet	a ball of rock and ice
meteor	the light trail of a burning meteoroid
meteorite	a meteoroid that has landed on a planet or moon's surface

ace **temperature** of a meteoroid may heat up to
°F (1,649°C) as it falls through Earth's atmosphere.

A BAD DAY FOR DINOSAURS

Many scientists believe that an asteroid 6 miles (9.7 km) wide hit Earth about 65 million years ago. As it headed to Earth, it created a huge fireball, burning nearly everything in its path. It landed in Mexico. The explosion the asteroid created was many times more powerful than all the atomic bombs in the world put together.

The impact sent **molten** rock and steam high into the air. Smoke and dust filled the air, blocking sunlight. Temperatures dropped, killing the dinosaurs.

OUT OF THIS WORLD!

Some astronomers think the asteroid may have actually been a comet since it was so big.

Some scientists think that 80 percent of things living on Earth may have died from the asteroid impact 65 million years ago.

13

CRATERS

The craters on the moon are examples of asteroid impacts. For many years, scientists believed that volcanoes, not asteroids, created the moon's craters. Craters don't last as long on Earth because the surface is always changing. Water washes away craters, and plants can cover them up.

Meteor Crater in Arizona is the best-known example of an asteroid crater on Earth. An asteroid collided with Earth at that spot about 50,000 years ago. Because it's in a desert, it hasn't been washed away or covered with trees.

OUT OF THIS WORLD!

The asteroid that created Meteor Crater was traveling at 26,000 miles (41,834 km) per hour. Meteor Crater is nearly 4,000 feet (1,219 m) across and over 550 feet (168 m) deep.

14

The Meteor Crater asteroid was made of iron and nickel.

15

POWERFUL PUNCH

A house-sized asteroid would be about as powerful as the bomb dropped on Hiroshima, Japan, during World War II. That's strong enough to flatten buildings within a mile of it. A mile-wide asteroid traveling at great speed would be 10 million times worse. One that size could wipe out most life on the planet.

A large asteroid impact on Earth would be terrible even in the ocean. An ocean impact would create huge waves that could wipe out entire coastlines and kill millions of people.

OUT OF THIS WORLD!

Despite the harm it did to Earth, the asteroid that wiped out the dinosaurs was actually small compared to some of the asteroids in our solar system.

It may seem like something out of a movie, but asteroids have hit Earth in the past.

RECENT IMPACTS

In 1908, an asteroid exploded over an unpopulated area of Siberia in Russia. The explosion flattened millions of trees over hundreds of miles. Had it exploded over a city, it would have killed thousands of people. This event shows that asteroids don't have to hit Earth's surface to cause great harm.

On October 9, 1992, a football-sized meteorite punched a hole through the trunk of a car in Peekskill, New York. The original meteoroid was much larger. Fortunately, most of it burned up before it landed.

OUT OF THIS WORLD!

In April 2012, a large meteor was seen over California and Nevada. Daylight makes most meteors very hard to see.

Peekskill
· · · · ·
Stone, chondrite (ordinary, H)
Fell 1992
Westchester County, New York

The Peekskill meteor was a bright fireball
that was seen in the sky over several states.

19

NEAR-EARTH OBJECTS

Asteroids, comets, or meteoroids that come close to Earth are called near-Earth objects. So far, astronomers have discovered almost 9,000 near-Earth objects. Scientists and astronomers use a combination of ground and space **telescopes** to track them.

Near-Earth objects that come very close to Earth are called potentially hazardous objects. This means it's possible the objects are dangerous, even if it's unlikely. Astronomers know of about 1,300 potentially hazardous objects. Improved telescopes could help find more near-Earth objects.

meteorite

Telescopes like this are used to search for asteroids and other space objects.

21

WHAT CAN WE DO?

If astronomers spot an asteroid on a collision course with Earth, what can we do? There are several ideas. One popular plan is to launch a **nuclear** bomb to blow up an approaching asteroid!

Some scientists think that trying to blow up an asteroid might be too risky. They're afraid that an explosion would break an asteroid into pieces, creating more asteroids headed for Earth. If the blast isn't big enough, the pieces of an asteroid may stay close together as they travel.

It's hard to know exactly where an asteroid or comet will hit until it's close to Earth.

23

BUMP IT

Instead of using a bomb to blow up an asteroid, it may be possible for an explosion to knock an asteroid off course. However, it would be very hard to time the explosion just right. The bomb might miss its target or just break apart the asteroid.

Another idea is to ram a spacecraft into the asteroid to bump it off course. In 2005, NASA (National Aeronautics and Space Administration) was able to crash a spacecraft into a comet so they could study it.

OUT OF THIS WORLD!

Tiny spacecraft called "mirror bees" are another idea. Their mirrors would use sunlight to heat an asteroid and change its course.

This photo shows the crash of NASA's *Deep Impact* spacecraft into comet Tempel 1 on July 4, 2005.

PULL IT OFF TRACK

Perhaps a better idea is to send a rocket to an asteroid—but not to blow it up. Instead, the rocket would orbit the asteroid. The orbiting rocket's gravity could slowly pull the asteroid off course. This kind of spacecraft is called a "gravity tractor."

On April 13, 2029, an asteroid named Apophis will pass very close to Earth. When it passes again in 2036, it may be close enough to be considered a potentially hazardous object. Until then, scientists will keep a close watch on it.

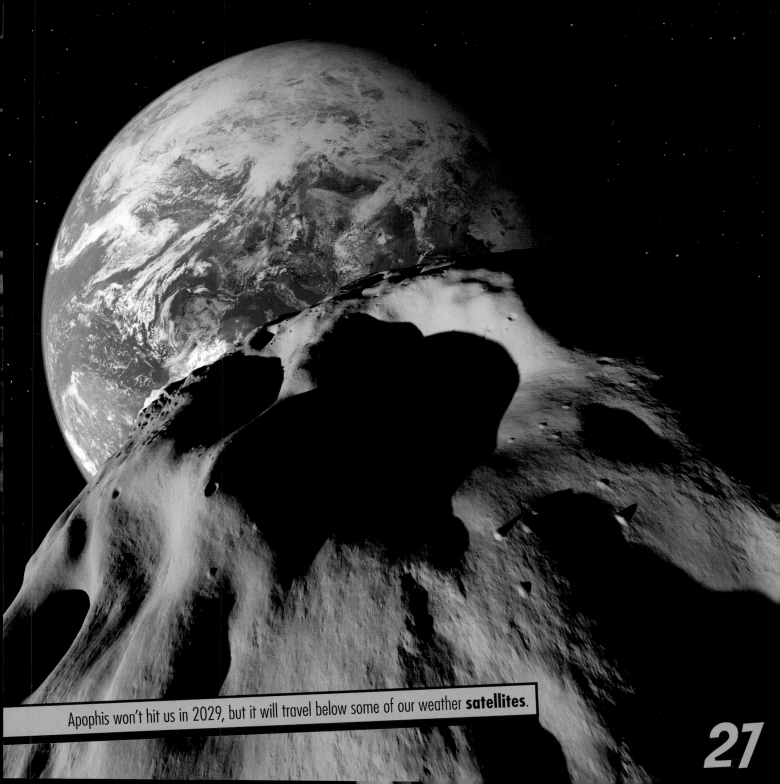

Apophis won't hit us in 2029, but it will travel below some of our weather **satellites**.

THE CLOCK IS TICKING

It's only a matter of time before another asteroid hits Earth. If it's big enough, it'll cause terrible harm or even destroy life as we know it. Fortunately, collisions with giant asteroids are very rare. After all, it's been about 65 million years since an asteroid wiped out the dinosaurs.

Currently there's no government program in place to stop an asteroid or comet of any size from hitting Earth. But astronomers will keep watching the skies in search of any danger.

OUT OF THIS WORLD!

NASA's *Dawn* spacecraft is orbiting the large asteroid Vesta. Some meteorites that have landed on Earth are pieces of Vesta.

This is an artist's idea of the *Dawn* spacecraft orbiting the giant asteroid Vesta.

29

GLOSSARY

astronomer: a person who studies stars, planets, and other heavenly bodies

debris: the remains of something that has been broken

friction: the force that slows motion between two objects touching each other

gravity: the force that pulls objects toward the center of a planet or star

impact: the action of one thing hitting another

molten: changed into a liquid form by heat

nuclear: having to do with the power created by splitting atoms, the smallest bits of matter

orbit: to travel in a circle or oval around something, or the path used to make that trip

satellite: an object that circles Earth in order to collect and send information or aid in communication

solar system: the sun and all the space objects that orbit it, including the planets and their moons

telescope: a tool that makes faraway objects look bigger and closer

temperature: how hot or cold something is

FOR MORE INFORMATION

BOOKS

Elkins-Tanton, Linda T. *Asteroids, Meteorites, and Comets*. New York, NY: Facts on File, 2010.

Kortenkamp, Steve. *Asteroids, Comets, and Meteoroids*. Mankato, MN: Capstone Press, 2012.

Schaaf, Fred. *The 50 Best Sights in Astronomy and How to See Them: Observing Eclipses, Bright Comets, Meteor Showers, and Other Celestial Wonders*. Hoboken, NJ: John Wiley, 2007.

WEBSITES

Asteroids
www.kidsastronomy.com/asteroid.htm
Learn more about the asteroids in our solar system.

Solar System Exploration
solarsystem.nasa.gov/kids/
Play games while learning about objects beyond Earth.

INDEX